The
Bushcraft Kid

ReadZone Books Limited

www.ReadZoneBooks.com

© in this edition 2016 ReadZone Books Limited

This print edition published in cooperation with Fiction Express, who first published this title in weekly instalments as an interactive e-book.

FICTION
EXPRESS

Fiction Express
First Floor Office, 2 College Street,
Ludlow, Shropshire SY8 1AN
www.fictionexpress.co.uk

Find out more about Fiction Express on pages 76–77.

Design: Laura Harrison & Keith Williams
Cover Image: Bigstock.com (ikopylov)

© in the text 2015 Jo Franklin
The moral right of the author has been asserted.

ISBN 978-1-78322-600-9

Printed in Malta by Melita Press

The Bushcraft Kid

Jo Franklin

What do other readers think?

Here are some comments left on the Fiction Express blog about this book:

"We are reading The Bushcraft Kid *and we love it."*
"Thank you for writing such an exciting story!"
Classes 7 and 8 Alexandra Park Primary School, Stockport

"I like this book because it's really funny and it's so cool."
Abby, London

"Hi Jo, your books are so cool. My hobby isn't really reading but now I am quite getting into your books! I have never read books that I like or get into so much it's so SURPRISING!!!"
Maryann, Canterbury

"It is a really good book. I love it sooo much. Can't wait to read more."
Abbi, Southall

"I like the book. It is so amazing because I like going camping in the rain and making fires."
Barneybear, Ketley

Contents

For Eleanor and Cedric, my own bushcraft kids.

Chapter 1

The Chase

I crouched in the dark shadows behind the bins. The sharp stink of rotting rubbish made my eyes sting. It wasn't the best place to hide, but I didn't have a choice – this estate was crawling with enemy agents. I had to get home without being caught.

I looked at my building, sussing it out. I could easily take the stairs in ninety-seven seconds but the light in the stairwell flickered, then went out. Someone or something was waiting, ready to pounce. I had to find another way up to my third-floor apartment.

As I peered out from my hiding place, a dark figure suddenly emerged from the shadows. He scanned the area, and kicked at an empty bottle. It spun across the tarmac, smacked against a skip and shattered. A few shards of glass flew at my legs but they didn't hurt me. I was wearing the army trousers recommended by Mr Wilderness. They were quick drying, thorn-proof and, it seemed, glass-proof too. Of course, Mr Wilderness meant them to be worn in the jungle, as part of a wilderness survival kit… but the city was just as dangerous.

It was already dark. The moon was hidden by the clouds, but street lights threw a murky yellow glow over the estate. I could survive outside all night if I wanted to, but my family would worry if I didn't get home soon.

Satisfied that the area was clear, the figure disappeared around the far side of the flats. It was time to move.

I slipped out of my hiding place into the shadows cast by the concrete walls. My khaki army clothes were designed to blend into any landscape. I was almost invisible, a stealth ninja flitting between the shadows.

A large skip was parked just beyond the staircase. It was stacked with old fridges and sofas, and topped by a double mattress. To some it was nothing but a rubbish dump, but to me it was a way home. I reckoned I could jump from the top of the pile to the first-floor balcony.

I scrambled into the skip as quietly as possible. Something squealed and three rats with long, bald tails scurried out of the rubbish into the night. The sound of heavy footfall echoed off the walls. Looking back, I watched in horror as a group of men rounded the corner. As one, they stopped and looked up. A sinister grin lit their faces. They'd found me.

With only seconds to get away, I leapt towards the railing. The cold metal cut into my hands but I gripped it tight and hauled myself up to the first floor. Sprinting along the balcony, I fled up the fire escape ladder.

As I made it to the third floor, I quickly glanced back. Were they still after me? I couldn't see them but the thud of enemy boots echoed up the stairwell. They were closing in. I took a running jump in the direction of my own balcony, landing with a roll.

I was home… safe. Nobody could hurt me here.

* * *

I looked over the railings, tracing my route with a satisfied smile. Everything was quiet....

There *were* no enemy agents of course. There never had been. I liked to set myself these imaginary challenges, to keep myself fit and develop my skills in case I ever needed them for real. The 'chase' was just a way to charge myself up – to get the best out of my freerunning.

Heading inside our flat, I dropped my bag on the floor and kicked off my running shoes.

"Hi Harley!" Mum was too busy cooking dinner to notice I hadn't used the front door.

"Your magazine came in the post." She pointed to the latest issue of *Bushcraft Times* on the counter. Wilderness survival and bushcraft was my other passion.

Mr Wilderness was on the cover with a group of kids.

SOUTH PEAKS
BUSHCRAFT COMPETITION

Sponsored by Southern TV News

First Prize: spend a weekend in the wild with **Mr Wilderness**.

A three-day race from one side of the South Peaks National Park to the other, using bushcraft skills to survive.

A survival competition! The kids on the cover were former winners. They looked tough, but I reckoned I could take them on. If I could make my escape with 'enemy agents' on my tail, I could survive anything. This was my chance to try out everything I'd ever learned from Mr Wilderness.

Chapter 2

The Competition

On the big day, we left our apartment so early it was still dark. Mum had been brilliant when I'd said I wanted to enter the competition. She'd bought me a new waterproof jacket and walking boots, so I could stay dry whatever the weather.

Finally, after a six-hour drive, we saw the rugged hills that gave the national park its name.

At the foot of the hills was a small village. A patchwork of slate roofs and stone cottages nestled in amongst green slopes, but as the hills rose steeper, the grass was replaced by bright yellow gorse bushes and purple heather. These then gave way to rocky outcrops and craggy peaks that seemed to stretch out forever into the distance. I'd studied loads of maps of the South Peaks National Park but nothing prepared me for how massive the hills looked up close. I'd lived in the city all my life – could I compete against real country kids to survive in this wilderness?

We pulled into the car park at the rangers' HQ and visitor centre and Mum squeezed my hand "Feeling nervous?" she asked.

"No way," I grinned, leaping out of the car. I checked that my trousers were tucked into my gaiters and pulled on my green beanie hat. I'd already smeared green and brown camouflage paint across my face so that every part of me would blend into the background. Pulling on my backpack, I was ready.

A large group of kids with numbers pinned to their chests were milling around. Some were wearing jeans. Anyone who knows anything about survival will tell you that wet jeans are the quickest way to hypothermia. But these fashion victims had dressed up for the TV cameras.

A few of my competitors were better prepared for the outdoors. I recognized some of them from the front cover of *Bushcraft Times*.

The kid wearing a number one wore matching black running leggings, T-shirt and trainers. He was doing leg stretches against a fence post until he saw me. Flicking his floppy fringe out of his eyes, he looked me up and down.

"Who are *you*?" he sneered. "The Bushcraft Kid?" He burst into howls of laughter.

"Reckon he can beat you, Finn?" Number Three grinned. He was also wearing running gear, but he had a Bart Simpson T-shirt with 'Eat My Shorts' thrown over the top.

"No one beats me, Jackson," Finn replied. "Especially not someone who wears makeup." He nodded his head towards me and I could feel my face burn red under my camouflage paint.

"Watch it, Finn Riley!" A girl with a brown ponytail pulled down her hood. She wore walking trousers and a sensible waterproof jacket a bit like mine. "I put mascara on today," she said.

"You won't beat me, Tasha. None of you will." Finn made out he was speaking to the crowd of competitors, but he fixed his eyes on me.

I knelt down and pretended to adjust my bootlaces. I didn't care what they said. This competition was about survival. I had watched every program Mr Wilderness had ever made. I'd read and memorised all his books. My skills and knowledge should see me through, even if the others had more field experience than me. Besides, I was determined – I was going to win this competition. And at the end I would make Finn Riley shake my hand.

* * *

The first stage of the competition was orienteering. We had to visit different checkpoints. There, we'd pick up tokens to swap for stuff we needed to make a camp that night. They didn't tell us what items we could have. I was hoping for a head torch, waterproof matches, a sleeping bag and a groundsheet.

"Take nothing in your rucksack except spare clothing, a water bottle and a flare," the chief ranger said. "If you get into difficulties light your flare and someone will find you. Water and food will be provided at the checkpoints. The first checkpoint is at the top of Grey Tor. You'll be able to collect your map and compass there so you can plan the rest of your route. Good luck." He blew his whistle and everyone started running.

One group made straight for the pile of rocks on the hill above the visitor centre. But I had studied the maps. I knew that there was a steep rock face immediately below the tor on this side. It was far too steep to climb without special equipment.

The quickest way to the top was from the south. This meant taking the path by the church on the other side of the village.

As I ran in that direction, I noticed Finn, Tasha and Jackson disappearing round the back of the rangers' office. Perhaps they knew a short cut....

Sticking to my plan, I vaulted the church gate and ran into the graveyard. There were loads of deep puddles, but I wasn't going to let a bit of water stop me.

Dashing between the tombstones, I headed for a stile in the corner. As I clambered over it I paused for a moment to get my bearings. That's when I saw the sign.

DANGER
Path Closed
Unstable Bridge

The way was blocked! How was I going to get to Grey Tor now? Another sign indicated a detour, but who knew how long that route would take?

Chapter 3

The Race is On

I stared at the warning sign, considering my options. On my estate I'd scaled vertical walls and leapt from rooftop to rooftop… I wasn't going to let a country bridge stop me now.

I vaulted the sign, crossed two muddy fields and sped towards two posts at the edge of the riverside. On the opposite bank were two more posts. In-between there was a big, empty gap. The bridge wasn't wobbly, it was non-existent!

The dark rocks of Grey Tor loomed

directly ahead and a light grey ribbon path wound its way up to the summit. I knew it was the fastest route, if only I could reach it. I couldn't go back to the start now. Somehow I had to cross the river.

The water below me was a raging torrent. The water thundered down, foaming and spitting as it hit the rocks that lined the river bed. The force of the current would sweep me right off my feet if I tried to wade or swim across.

Further upstream, a tree arched over the river, pointing its skeletal fingers towards a shark-fin rock in the middle. Between this boulder and the opposite bank was a flat ledge covered with shallower water.

Three obstacles between me and my target. How difficult could it be?

I closed my eyes for a moment and imagined enemy agents behind me, only this time they looked like Finn and Jackson. I soon had the familiar feeling of adrenalin pumping through my veins. There was no way I was going to let Finn and Jackson get the better of me. I *was* the Bushcraft Kid and I was going to win this competition.

Rushing over to the tree, I leapt up and grabbed the low branch. I hurriedly edged forward, swinging my legs out over the gushing water. The tree began to groan as it supported my weight. The water swirled and hissed as it rushed beneath me. It was almost alive. An icy monster flicking freezing wet tentacles at my legs.

My toes touched the jagged rock just as a loud crack splintered the air. Half he tree crashed down and disappeared in a rush of foamy water, but I had let go and was now teetering on the edge of the shark's fin trying to work out what to do next.

The ledge I'd spotted earlier now looked much further away but I had to go for it. I judged the distance and launched my weight forward and landing cat-like on the flat rock.

For a moment I thought all was well as I straightened up. But before I knew what was happening, one foot shot out from under me and I landed, hard, on my side. As I began to slip from the ledge, I realized it was covered in slimy moss. Almost the same colour as the stone, it had been invisible from a distance. Now most of my body was in the river.

I groped in the icy water and managed to find a handhold. The raging torrent tried to rip me downstream, but I managed to steady myself using a hand grip I had practised many times during freerunning. Carefully placing my feet back on the slippery stone, I tensed and sprang again, landing with a thud on the riverbank.

Awesome – I'd made it!

But I was also soaking wet. Even my backpack was drenched, meaning that my emergency flare would be useless. If Mum was here, she'd tell me to give up now, that it was too dangerous, that I needed a flare in case I got into difficulties. But she wasn't a freerunning, bushcraft loving, adrenalin junkie like me. I had a race to complete.

* * *

The path was easy to follow and my clothing began to dry off quickly in the sun. That's why I wasn't wearing jeans. Quick-drying clothes were essential for survival in the wilderness. In less than ten minutes I was standing on the top of Grey Tor. I had completed the first stage… but Finn Riley had beaten me to it.

"Been swimming, bush boy?" he sneered at my damp trousers. He stuffed a map into his rucksack and ran on before I could answer.

"Next up, orienteering," the ranger said to me. "There are six coloured boxes containing tokens. Collect three different tokens and bring them back here. You'll be able to swap them for essentials to get you through the night ahead. If you don't complete the task before nightfall, set off your flare. It'll be the end of the competition for you."

"Okay," I said. "But I think my flare might be ruined." I unzipped my rucksack… but there was no flare inside. "That's weird! I put it in here at the start."

"Lucky for you I've got a spare," the ranger said. "But don't lose this one. It could save your life."

I nodded and shoved it in my bag hoping I wouldn't need it. Then I studied the map, selected the three nearest checkpoints and chose my route.

First stop – blue box.

Chapter 4

Sabotage

As I ran, I thought about the missing flare. I had definitely put it into my rucksack with my water bottle. Someone must have taken it out. But who? I wanted to win, but I would never put other people in danger to do it. This competition was hard enough.

The blue orienteering box peeked out from a pile of rocks ahead. As I scrambled up, I saw Finn rushing down the other side. I was gaining on him.

I flipped open the lid but the blue box was totally empty! Finn must have taken all the tokens. All the other competitors, including me, were going to have to find other boxes to complete the challenge. What a cheat!

I checked the map again. There was no point following Finn – he was sure to take every token he could find. I decided to head for the yellow box. According to the map it was in a woodland on the far side of the hill. Finn wouldn't have time to get there before me.

The rocky path gave way to a carpet of pine needles and I was grateful for the softness of the woodland floor as I ran into the trees. My soggy boots were beginning to rub blisters.

A yellow knotted rope hung from a tall pine ahead. A climbing challenge!

The box was nailed to the tree about ten metres above me. I grabbed hold of the rope and began to climb. It was much harder than it looked. Rope climbing hadn't been part of urban freerunning training, but I was soon in a rhythm. Even though the rope swung wildly like a mad snake below me, I was soon parallel to the yellow box.

I wrapped my legs around the rope and reached out to get a token. But suddenly the rope jolted. Above me, strands of yellow stuck out at all angles from the main rope. It creaked and another loose thread popped out. The rope was snapping. I was going to fall!

I grasped the tree trunk and I transferred my weight onto a branch, just as the last strand broke and the rope fell to the ground. Balancing carefully, I reached out and claimed my yellow token.

One down, two to go.

Luckily the tree was studded with sawn off limbs which were easy to use as a ladder. Much simpler than using the rope. I don't know why I didn't climb the tree in the first place.

When I reached the ground, I picked up the rope and studied the end. Someone had definitely cut through it. The saboteur had struck again!

A twig snapped and I looked up. Tasha stood a few metres away.

"You'll have to climb the tree," I told her. "I think someone cut the rope."

Tasha grinned, flashed a yellow token at me and ran away into the woods.

Now it looked like Tasha was the saboteur. Maybe she was working with Finn.

This was a nightmare. The competition was hard enough without battling against a bunch of cheats. I took out my map and compass. The only way to win this race was to go to the orienteering points furthest from the finish. The saboteurs were lazy. They wanted to win without making an effort.

I ran in the opposite direction to Tasha and, after working out the route on the map, found the purple box. It was full of tokens, so Finn the cheat hadn't been here yet. I took mine and hurried on.

I couldn't understand why people wanted to wreck the competition. For me, this was about challenging myself as much as racing against the others. I didn't want to cheat my way to the cover of *Bushcraft Times*. And I was sure Mr Wilderness wouldn't want that either!

When I left the woods the sun was low in the sky. It would be evening soon. I had to find another token and get back to

Grey Tor before sundown or it would all be over.

I followed a grassy trail that I hoped led to the red box. The South Peaks National Park was a beautiful place. The low sunbeams lit up the subtle purple hues of the heather. Bright splashes of acid yellow gorse shone out like polished gold. I planned to return to South Peaks when I had more time to look at everything in detail.

At last I saw the red box ahead. There were plenty of tokens inside. I added one to my collection and headed back to Grey Tor.

The sky was beginning to turn pink as the sun slipped towards the horizon. A thin sliver of moon appeared. It was going to be a dark night.

* * *

Three contestants beat me to the top of Grey Tor – Finn, Jackson and Tasha. I hurried past them towards the ranger to exchange my tokens.

"Well done," he said. "Any problems?"

"Loads!" I explained. "Someone stole all the blue tokens, and the climbing rope at the yellow checkpoint was cut through. Somebody's sabotaging the competition!"

"There *is* no rope at the yellow checkpoint," the ranger said. "That's a tree-climbing task."

"But there was a rope," I insisted. "And what about the blue tokens?"

"You needed to get to the box first to guarantee a token," the man shrugged. "There weren't enough for you all – not everyone can make it through to the next round. This is a competition, you know," he said with a wink.

I could see there was no point in arguing, so I handed over my tokens. The ranger gave me a camping saucepan containing a sealed pouch of pasta in tomato sauce, a banana and a carton of apple juice.

"Now, you get to choose your pack," he said." You'll be spending the night outside and cooking that meal for yourself… so choose wisely."

I looked at the options before me.

First, there was a tent which would give me immediate shelter. That meant I could concentrate on making a fire and cooking the food.

The second pack contained matches, cotton wool and Vaseline in a waterproof bag. That would be the easiest way to start a fire in the wilderness, giving me more time to make a shelter and collect fire wood.

Finally, there was a backpack identical to the one Mr Wilderness takes with him on his adventures… but with no indication of what was inside.

This was going to be a difficult decision!

Chapter 5

Against the Elements

Mr Wilderness says there are three priorities for survival – shelter, warmth and food. The food had been provided by the ranger, but now I had to choose between shelter and warmth. I wanted them both.

As Finn, Tasha and Jackson headed off, I turned my attention back to the options in front of me. The mystery pack was tempting. It looked exactly like the one Mr Wilderness had on his last television series… but what was inside?

As there was no way of knowing, I decided it was too much of a risk. So it was a choice between the tent and the fire-making equipment.

It was already getting dark and a thick band of cloud hugged the horizon. If it was going to rain, I needed shelter. So the tent looked like a good option. Cavemen had survived without matches and cotton wool, so I reckoned I could find a different way to start a fire.

Another competitor dashed up behind me… it was time to make my choice. I reached for the tent.

"I see you're not a gambler," the ranger said, pointing to the mystery pack on the table. "Don't forget to light your flare if you get into trouble."

"Thanks, but I'll be fine!" I turned and set off to make camp.

I decided to head for the woods. I wasn't sure I'd get a comfortable night sleeping on the rocky summit of Grey Tor.

On my way I found a few things that would come in handy for starting a fire. The silky seed heads from a wild clematis were fine and dry and would make perfect tinder. I picked up a few fir cones to use as kindling and there were loads of dead trees in the woods, which would make the main fuel for a fire. If only I had a light. I stored the items carefully in my backpack.

The scent of wood smoke wafted through the trees. Someone else must have chosen the matches or maybe they had used another method of starting a fire.

Following the smell, it was easy to find the camper. Jackson sat hunched over a pile of twigs in front of a tent. Despite the smoke, I couldn't see a single flame.

"Your sticks are too wet," I said. "You need dry wood to get a fire going."

"Right, yeah… thanks for the tip," said Jackson.

"I see you chose the tent," I said. "But how did you strike a spark to start your fire?"

"Err, the old 'rubbing two sticks together' technique," smiled Jackson. As he acted out the motion with his hands, I noticed that he scraped his boot in the soft leaf litter at his feet. Was that a glint of metal I'd seen?

"Uh-huh…" I said, unconvinced. "Well, I'd better go and set up camp!"

"Watch out – it looks like rain," replied Jackson looking up. I grimaced. The night sky was now heavy with rain clouds.

* * *

Deep within the woods I found an area that had been cleared to make a picnic site. There was a circle of grass, a picnic bench and a litter bin. Not exactly the wilderness I had imagined, but it wasn't against the rules to camp here either.

A rising breeze signalled the start of a storm. I needed to get my tent up as soon as possible.

First I trampled the grass down and laid the tent out flat as best I could with the wind catching at the material. I slotted the flexible poles together and eventually managed to feed them through the sleeves in the tent material.

As I worked, I felt raindrops on the back of my neck. Placing my tent in position, I stashed my food and rucksack inside, just as the heavens opened.

I pulled my hood up, desperate to keep the rain from dripping down my neck.

I hooked the first tent peg into a guy rope and tried to push it into the ground. But the clearing was a compacted mass of grass and tree roots.

Somehow I had to find a makeshift hammer. With ever-stronger gusts of wind, it was essential to pin my tent down and to keep the fabric taut so that the rain ran off.

Suddenly there was a whooshing sound and a bright light drifted down from the sky. Someone had set of their flare – they'd given up. I wasn't going to let a bit of rain beat me!

Glancing around, I spotted a stone on the other side of the clearing that looked large and heavy enough to do the job. I ran directly towards it, vaulting the litter bin on the way.

The stone was stuck fast in the matted grass. My fingers were numb with cold and the rain made it hard to get a good grip. But eventually I managed to work the rock free.

I now had an excellent hammer. Five minutes later all the pegs were secure in the ground and my tent was finally up.

I collapsed inside, grateful to be out of the rain at last.

Chapter 6

A Helping Hand

I didn't stand a chance of lighting a fire now. My tinder and kindling were dry enough in my rucksack, but they weren't any good on their own. I had no choice but to eat my supper cold out of the packet.

I was about to start on the banana when I heard a voice outside.

"Anybody home?" A ranger shone a torch into my tent. "Are you happy to carry on overnight?"

"Absolutely," I said. "I'm a bit damp, but I'll live,"

"I brought you these." The ranger handed me a torch, a flask and a sleeping bag. "Didn't think we'd leave you to freeze tonight, did you?"

"Err, kind of," I said. "Thanks!"

"No problem. See you tomorrow." With that, he disappeared into the wet night.

The flask was warm and, when I opened it, the strong scent of cocoa wafted out. That hot chocolate must have had magical properties. It changed me from being cold and fed up, to being the happiest camper on the planet.

I hung up my damp clothes inside the tent and got ready for bed. The sleeping bag felt like a heavenly cocoon when I slipped inside.

The ground was hard and the rain drummed heavily on the waterproof fabric of my tent. Despite this, I was asleep in minutes, dreaming of floating away on a sea of chocolatey milk.

* * *

I think I would have slept forever but I was woken suddenly in the night. Something outside was trying to destroy my tent. Or trying to get into the tent with me. I was too confused to know which.

The front flap was zipped open and a torch beam shone out of the blackness into my face.

"I'm going to kill you Finn Riley!" A shrill voice screamed. It sounded like Tasha.

"I'm not Finn," I said sleepily. "I'm Harley."

"Oh," Tasha lowered her torch. "Sorry… don't suppose you saw where he set up camp, did you?"

"No," I said. "I haven't seen him since the three of you were up at the tor."

"He's sabotaged my camp. I woke to find my tarpaulin tent slashed, my fire stamped out and my stash of wood gone." Tasha sank to her knees inside my tent.

"You had a tarpaulin?" I was struggling to make sense of what she was saying.

"Yeah, I chose the mystery pack," explained Tasha. "I got a tarpaulin and a flint strike-a-light. For once I struck gold and made the perfect camp… but Finn ruined it."

I was fully awake now. A strike-a-light was the foolproof way to start a fire. Even though I was snug in my sleeping bag, my clothes were still wet and I had to wear them tomorrow. A fire was exactly what I needed.

"I don't know what to do," she sighed.

Chapter 7

A Disturbed Night

I felt sorry for Tasha. Should I invite her to share my tent in exchange for a fire? But then, this was a competition – perhaps I should be more ruthless.

Suddenly I pictured Tasha smirking beside the broken yellow rope. She had looked so triumphant then, but now she looked half broken. She drew her hands up into the sleeves of her fleece and wrapped her arms around her knees.

"Why would Finn wreck my camp like that?" she groaned. "I just don't get it."

"What will you do if you find *his* camp?" I said. "Trash that, too?"

Tasha shook her head. "That's not my style. I might fill his walking boots with water though." A tired smile flitted across her face. "I love these bushcraft challenges, but Finn and Jackson have ruined the whole thing by being so competitive. There's no need to cheat to have a good time."

"So it wasn't you that cut the rope on the tree then? Or took all the tokens?" I sat up straighter in my sleeping bag, eager to hear what she had to say.

"No!" She sounded outraged. "If I'd seen you climbing I'd have warned you, too. I didn't realize you were up there! To be honest, I don't care if I win or lose as long as I complete the course."

"That's how I feel, too," I said, and suddenly I knew exactly what I was going to do. "Finn was totally out of order trashing your camp like that. You shouldn't be forced into giving up the competition. Look what I picked up earlier." I rummaged in my rucksack and took out the dry fire-making materials. "Do you still have the strike-a-light?"

Tasha's face brightened and she showed me the metal stick and flat plate that had been in her mystery pack.

"Why don't we join forces?" I suggested. "It's stopped raining. We could light a fire outside the tent. I could dry my clothes and keep an eye out for the saboteur while you get some sleep in the tent. We could swap over in a few hours."

"That's a brilliant idea." A look of relief washed over Tasha's face. "We'll have to go our separate ways in the morning though, otherwise we might be disqualified."

"No problem," I said, "though I don't remember any rules about not working together."

"Right, well, I'll go and find some dry firewood," beamed Tasha.

"I'll join you once I'm dressed," I said.

* * *

It's easy to make a fire when you have the right materials. First we made a safe site by ripping out the grass outside the tent to form a square metre of bare earth. Then we made a circle of stones and, inside it, a platform of small sticks we'd found. This would protect our tinder from getting damp and would allow air to get to the fire.

I shaped the dry clematis heads into a nest with a sprinkle of crumbled fir cone and then built a wigwam of small, brittle sticks above it. Tasha scraped the two parts of the strike-a-light together and a tiny spark flew out. It took two or three goes but then the tinder began to glow. Soon, a tiny flame flickered up into the sticks, which in turn caught light. We carefully fed more sticks into the fire until we had a real blaze going. "It's one o'clock now," I said. "I think you should get some sleep."

Tasha didn't need to be asked twice. She disappeared into the tent leaving me alone in the darkness. I didn't care. I wanted to savour the moment, enjoying the heat from my first real bushcraft fire.

The fire crackled and hissed as the flames consumed the dead wood. I could see why Mr Wilderness loved this life. It was fantastic to pit your own skills and strength against the wild. This challenge wasn't over, but I already wanted to do it again.

Snap! A branch broke in the darkness.

"Is that you, Finn?" I shouted.

Someone laughed. A dark shape moved in amongst the shadowy trees at the edge of the picnic area. I thought I saw of flash of yellow in the darkness.

"What is it?" Tasha poked her head out of the tent.

"I couldn't tell. It might have been Finn," I replied. "Or even Jackson," I added, remembering the Bart Simpson T-shirt he'd been wearing. "Could it have been *him* that trashed your camp?"

Before she could answer, a large branch flew out of the pitch black towards us. It smashed onto the grass in front of me, just missing our fire and sending twig fragments and leaves flying into the air.

"Idiot!" Tasha yelled but no one answered. Whoever it was had gone.

Chapter 8

A Bad Sign

Tasha and I shared the task of keeping watch, but the saboteur didn't come back. In the morning we were both reasonably refreshed and wearing warm, dry clothes.

Thanks for your help," Tasha said. "But let's keep it between you and me – just in case." She headed off to the day's briefing.

I knew she was right, but a part of me also wondered if we would need to join forces again against the mystery saboteur. After all, we both wanted to get to the end and meet Mr Wilderness tomorrow.

*　*　*

When I arrived at the briefing, we were told there were only eight of us left in the competition. Finn and Jackson stood beside Tasha, along with four other competitors. Everyone else had dropped out, or, I suspected, been forced out by the saboteur.

The rangers had laid on a breakfast feast for us. Finn and Jackson sat at one end of the table stuffing their faces with bacon sandwiches. Tasha was slicing a banana over a huge bowl of muesli. I selected a healthy breakfast similar to Tasha's and sat down at the far end of the table.

The ranger congratulated us on getting this far in the competition and then told us what lay ahead.

"Today is more about endurance than skill," he said. "You need to follow the waymarked path of the Granite Trail until you get to the youth hostel at Gablehurst." He pointed at a place on a big map. "No map. No compass. No refuelling on route. You can take whatever food you want from the table, but remember you have to carry it. The only rule is you must take two litres of water with you. This isn't a race. Everyone who reaches the finish line will spend a comfortable night in the hostel and will be ready to face the final challenge tomorrow. Any questions?"

"How many bacon sandwiches will fit in my backpack?" Jackson said as he leapt up and cleared half the food from the table into his bag. Then he was off without saying 'thank you' or 'goodbye'. He ran straight to the start of the trail and disappeared out of sight. Finn and Tasha soon followed him.

There were no bacon sandwiches left, but I didn't care. I knew the salty meat would make me thirsty, which was the last thing I wanted on an endurance test. I settled for a juicy apple, a banana and a few slices of buttered wholemeal bread.

The Granite Way was a wide path that followed the backbone of the South Peaks National Park. The ground fell away steeply on one side. Narrow sheep tracks left the main path now and again and disappeared amongst the rocks. The slope on the other side was gentler. It was clothed with grass and wild flowers, which danced in the breeze. I didn't know the names of the flowers, but next time I came here I would bring a book with me and look them up. I wanted to know as much about the countryside as Mr Wilderness.

After two or three hours of jogging and walking, I came to the brow of a hill. A crooked signpost drunkenly indicated the way to Gablehurst and a place called Down's Hollow. That sounded like a valley to me, but the sign was pointing along the main path. Meanwhile the sign for the Granite Trail and Gablehurst pointed down a steep track to the left.

I saw a small figure trotting in that direction.

"Hey Tasha," I yelled.

Without turning, she raised her hand in acknowledgement. Then, with a sharp scream, she disappeared. She was in trouble!

As I charged towards the top off the path, my rucksack caught on the signpost. It toppled to the ground, nearly taking me with it. Then it was obvious. Someone had deliberately turned the signpost around to send us in the wrong direction.

I hurried on. "Tasha! Are you okay? Tasha!" My heart hammered against my ribcage as I scanned the rocky hillside looking for her.

"I'm here." A faint whimper came from a few metres further on. The ground fell away into what looked like a small quarry, half hidden by overhanging grass.

Tasha lay in a crumpled heap at the bottom, her leg sticking out at a funny angle.

She'd taken the wrong path because the sign had been moved and now she was seriously hurt. The sabotage was getting out of hand and I didn't have a clue what to do next.

Chapter 9

Meeting Mr Wilderness

"Don't move! I'm coming down to help you!" I yelled as I circled round to a narrow path at the side of the quarry "Careful, Harley!" Tasha called out. "It's really steep."

Loose grit rolled out from under my feet, clattered down the path ahead of me and disappeared into the abyss. The path came to an abrupt end. I peered over. Trees clung precariously to the edge of the precipice, bare roots hanging in the air like ragged washing on a clothesline. There must have been a landslip in the past, which had swept the soil and path away. Turning around and getting onto my hands and knees I managed to scramble down to join Tasha.

"That signpost! Somebody must have moved it," she spluttered, as she tried to pull herself upright. "That… that idiot, Finn Riley, I bet!" She was so cross she could barely speak.

"Don't worry about that now. We need to get you out of here." I knelt down and ran my hand along her lower leg. I knew nothing about first aid but I hoped that pretending I did might calm her down. "Do you think your leg is broken?'

"No, just twisted," Tasha sighed. "I'm more angry than hurt. That was a mean trick to play."

"Sure was. Do you want me to set off your flare? Get the rangers here?" I asked.

"No way! I'm going to finish this competition, even if I have to hop over the finish line," she said, a determined look on her face. "Can you help me up?"

"Take my hand." I said, hauling her upright. She couldn't put her weight on her bad leg but managed to scrabble up the steep side with my help. At the top, she draped her arm over my shoulders and we hobbled back to the main path together.

When we reached the sign, I pulled it upright and made sure it was pointing the right way again.

In a woody area we managed to find a piece of hazel that served as a walking stick. But the journey to Gablehurst was a slow one. It was a good job there was no time limit on the task.

As we drew close to the youth hostel, Tasha asked me not to tell the rangers what had happened. She didn't want the adults to get all 'Health and Safety' on us and cancel the competition. She wanted one of us to beat Finn Riley and teach him a lesson once and for all. I didn't feel very comfortable about it, but she was the one who had been hurt, so in the end I agreed.

When we arrived at the hostel she limped off to see the first aider while I had a quick bite to eat and then collapsed into bed. Helping a friend can be very tiring!

* * *

"Good morning, everybody!" Mr Wilderness stood in front of the remaining contestants with a big smile on his face. He was much shorter than he was on television, but it was brilliant to see him at last.

"Well done for surviving the competition this far. There are just four of you now, right? Er … Tasha, Finn, Jackson and Harley. Now it's time for the final challenge. Are you ready?" he asked.

"Bring it on!" Jackson stood up and punched the air.

Tasha looked over at me and rolled her eyes.

"You okay?" I mouthed.

She gave me the thumbs up and turned back to the briefing.

"Your final task is to build a raft and race it down the river," Mr Wilderness said. "Only rule is you have to wear a lifejacket. There'll be goodie bags for everyone at the end, but the winner is heading for the trip of a lifetime, so I hope your passports are up to date."

Passports? Was the prize a trip *abroad* with Mr Wilderness? My stomach flipped somersaults until I felt sick.

I'd only read about raft building. I'd never actually made one, but I knew I just had to cross that finish line first.

The rangers had created a pile of junk we could use to build our rafts. Jackson and Finn made a beeline for a stack of large plastic barrels and the longest planks of wood. Tasha was more interested in nets full of empty plastic water bottles, but I wasn't convinced that I needed that amount of buoyancy. There were no rapids or weirs on the river here, but there were rocks, which might snag those barrels and nets. I figured that a sleek, low raft would be easier to manoeuvre and would travel faster if it picked up a strong current.

I left the others and sifted through a pile of poles stacked in the corner. In amongst them were loads of massive bamboo canes. They were as thick as my arm, much bigger than the ones growing in our garden, but they were still light and strong. And they were hollow, which would help keep me afloat.

I laid my poles and bamboos on the ground side by side, with the longest one sticking out of the middle like the prow of a boat. Then I lashed them together with lengths of nylon rope.

"What're you making, Bushcraft Boy," Jackson sneered, "a bird cage?"

I ignored him, concentrating on the task in hand. I plastered mud into the open ends of the bamboo poles. I grabbed two flat boards to use as paddles and a long stick to use as a punt-pole. Once I'd checked my knots again, my raft was ready.

Chapter 10

Race to the Finish

The cameras from Southern TV News were lined up on the riverbank, ready to film everyone taking to the water. Jackson and Finn had built the biggest rafts. They looked very impressive on dry land but they both had trouble dragging them to the water's edge.

"Out of my way!" Jackson grunted as he pushed Finn to one side. He hauled his raft onto the river. It floated well, but the barrels were so big that when he stood up, his paddle barely skimmed the water.

Tasha was next, followed by Finn. As he pushed his raft into the water, lengths of rope trailed behind him in the mud.

"I think there's something wrong, mate!" I yelled, but he totally ignored me and paddled out into the middle of the river. "Your loss," I muttered under my breath.

My raft was no more than a platform, so it was easy to lift onto the water. It floated beautifully, and even when I stepped aboard it barely wobbled. I used my punt-pole to shove off from the riverbank, but then switched to a paddle. I knelt down and struck out into the main flow.

The river had seemed sleepy from the bank, but in the centre there was a strong current. It was thrilling to feel the wind against my face as I sped downriver.

I could see Finn up ahead. His raft was tilting at a precarious angle and he was struggling to stay on board. I knew those loose ropes were bad news – he was in real trouble. I couldn't see any rangers on the bank so I paddled furiously towards him.

"You okay?" I called out.

"Someone's slashed my ropes. The barrels are coming loose," Finn shouted. "I'm going d-ow-ow-n!" With that, one corner of his raft submerged and the other end rose up, tipping Finn into the river. Luckily he was wearing his lifejacket.

I lay flat on my raft and held my wooden paddle out to him. Finn grabbed it and scrambled aboard.

"Why didn't you leave me?" he said as he wiped his wet hair out of his eyes.

"Couldn't do that, mate." I replied. "If bushcraft isn't about helping others in distress, I don't know what it is."

Finn looked very guilty. "Look," he said. "I know you saw me taking all those tokens. That was a pretty dumb thing to do. I'm sorry."

"Yeah, that *was* dumb. But the other stuff was dangerous," I said, steering the raft back into the centre of the river.

"What *other* stuff?" Finn seemed surprised.

"The yellow rope trick, trashing Tasha's camp, switching the sign towards a dangerous path," I listed all the saboteur's tricks.

"What?! That wasn't me." Finn sounded genuinely shocked. "Someone trashed my camp too… I thought they were only messing with me. I didn't realize they were wrecking everything. There's a complete idiot in this competition somewhere."

"An idiot that's about to win," I said pointing at the figure standing tall on his raft downstream.

"Jackson, I might have known. We can't let him win," Finn said. "Maybe Tasha will beat him."

"I don't think so." I gestured at a figure in the water nearby. Tasha was bobbing about desperately trying to hold together the water bottles that used to be part of her raft. I steered towards her.

"Jackson slashed my nets as he went passed," she said. "He's a total cheat."

So Jackson had a knife. He'd used it to create sparks to light his fire the first night, he'd cut through the yellow rope and now he'd sabotaged the rafts.

"Grab your oar and climb aboard," I said. "Hopefully with the three of us paddling we should be able to catch him."

Finn and Tasha were soaked but they weren't ready to give up. They took positions at the front of the raft and paddled like crazy. I stayed at the back using my paddle to steer.

"This is an awesome craft," Finn said.

"Thanks," I replied with a small smile.

Jackson was still ahead of us but we were gaining on him. While we kept low on our raft, he was standing upright. He seemed to have lost his paddle and was relying on the current to carry him towards the finish line. He was shouting and waving at the TV cameras on the riverbank so he didn't see us approaching from behind.

As our raft zipped past him, a small wake formed. Jackson's top-heavy raft rose on the wave and, because he hadn't seen it coming, he was knocked off balance. Toppling over, he landed with a massive splash in the river. His raft bobbed away from him and came to a halt in amongst some reeds.

Jackson let out a soggy scream but Finn, Tasha and I didn't take any notice. Even in bushcraft there's no reason to help a saboteur!

Our raft sped across the finish line in a flurry of flashing cameras and cheering onlookers. We had won!

The rangers shoved hot drinks into our hands and draped silver survival blankets over our shoulders. I didn't need a blanket as I hadn't got wet, but I took one anyway. I hoped they'd let me take it home with me at the end of the day, as it was something I had always wanted.

"These kids have shown real strength of character this weekend," Mr Wilderness announced to the television cameras. "This was a serious challenge involving survival skills and stamina. I've been so impressed with the winners that I would like to award the main prize to all three. Harley, Tasha and Finn would you like to join me for a bushcraft weekend in Iceland during the school holidays next month?"

The three of us jumped into the air yelling. "Yes!"

"There is only one trophy though. Who should I award this year's South Peaks Bushcraft Cup to?" Mr Wilderness looked at the three of us expectantly.

"Harley!" Tasha and Finn said together, and they pushed me in front of the cameras.

That short walk was the most terrifying thing I had done in my life. My legs felt like a couple of rubber bands, but, somehow I summoned the strength to step up and accept the trophy from my hero on behalf of my new team. I looked around and saw Mum in the crowd, waving frantically. I grinned and waved back.

I felt awesome, but the best bit was knowing that we were all going to do it again. Next time we would have Mr Wilderness to help us. Imagine. Iceland! Volcanoes, waterfalls, geysers. The land of fire and ice. I'd always wanted to go there. Now that would be a *real* test of my bushcraft skills.

THE END

FICTI●N EXPRESS

THE READERS TAKE CONTROL!

Have you ever wanted to change the course of a plot, change a character's destiny, tell an author what to write next?

Well, now you can!

'The Bushcraft Kid' was originally written for the award-winning interactive e-book website Fiction Express.

Fiction Express e-books are published in gripping weekly episodes. At the end of each episode, readers are given voting options to decide where the plot goes next. They vote online and the winning vote is then conveyed to the author who writes the next episode, in real time, according to the readers' most popular choice.

www.fictionexpress.co.uk

WINNER
Education Resources
Award for Innovation

FICTI😮N EXPRESS

TALK TO THE AUTHORS

The Fiction Express website features a blog where readers can interact with the authors while they are writing. An exciting and unique opportunity!

FANTASTIC TEACHER RESOURCES

Each weekly Fiction Express episode comes with a PDF of teacher resources packed with ideas to extend the text.

"The teaching resources are fab and easily fill a whole week of literacy lessons!"
Rachel Humphries, teacher at Westacre Middle School

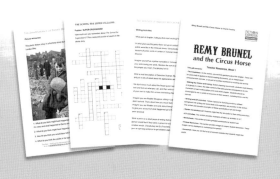

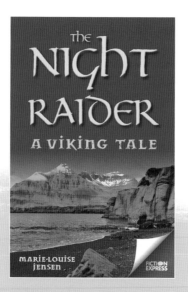

About the Author

Jo Franklin was born reading sometime in the last century. As a child, she loved making up stories but unfortunately no one could read her writing. Then Jo learned to touch-type and her life changed forever and she became a professional author. Her books have now been translated and published in other countries.

Jo likes to write about geeks, tomboys, aliens and other misfits. She sends them on crazy adventures so that they can discover how brilliant they are and that the world can't do without them.

Jo lives in South London with her family, two cats and a mad dog called Mickey. When she isn't writing, she spends her time hanging out in Peckham library, devising new filing systems for her study and chasing after a dog that never comes back. She loves chocolate and stationery but hates spiders.

You can find out more about Jo, her books and her mad dog at her website: www.jofranklinauthor.co.uk